A
MOST
MYSTERIOUS
MOUSE

Giovanna Zoboli • Lisa D'Andrea

Translated from the Italian by Antony Shugaar

ENCHANTED LION BOOKS
NEW YORK

Once upon a time there was a cat.
He was a handsome tabby cat,
with a head full of mice.

Indeed, he thought about mice all day long.

Sometimes he would think
about just one mouse,
which he would see
in great detail.

This happened on days
when he felt like a very precise cat.

At other times, he'd think about two mice together, but could see only one from head to tail.

The other remained a little blurry, as if he'd sailed into a cloud or was taking a steam bath to cure a cold.

This usually happened if the cat needed sleep or one of his ears was stopped up.

At still other times, he might see **THIRTY-THREE** mice dancing the polka.
This happened on days when he wished someone would invite him to a party.

The cat also liked to imagine a pack of **SIXTEEN** mice playing cards.
This usually happened towards evening, after daydreams in which he rode his bike
past a park where people were playing chess and tossing balls.

Sometimes he saw **TWENTY-SEVEN** mice
all lining up to buy a pair of rain boots made by the famous *Dr. Knapp*.

This happened on mornings when he was snug and warm in his bed,
but knew it was raining from the sounds outside.

He might also see **EIGHTY-EIGHT** mice in checkered jackets. This happened when his neighbor was belting out

SINGIN' IN THE RAIN

But if his ears were ringing from the roar of traffic,
then he liked to imagine **ONE HUNDRED AND FORTY-FOUR**
mice zooming along on a triple-decker bus.

Sometimes his friends would drop by to invite him out.
"You coming fishing?" they'd ask over the intercom.

"Not today," he'd reply.
"I'm far too busy thinking
about mice."

"Still?" they would ask,
impressed that he never
seemed to stop.

"Yes," he'd reply. "They're relying on me, you know."

And if someone asked him to go
snail hunting, he'd say,

"Maybe tomorrow. Right now, I have a whole new mouse in mind."

For this singular cat was also a very ambitious cat. And his promise to himself was that by his eighteenth birthday he would have imagined

1 *Million* mice.

This was his dream on especially hopeful days,
when he lay around indoors, thinking about the future.

On other days, he'd examine his conscience:

If I don't think about them, who will?
he'd ask himself.

This tended to happen when he was sitting up straight at his table,
looking himself in the eye and feeling dutiful.

He had already thought of so many different mice.

There was the mouse who cooked eggs.

The one with the crooked tail.

The one wearing a hat.

The one with a left foot bigger than his right.

The one who struggled to learn foreign languages.

The one in a bad mood.

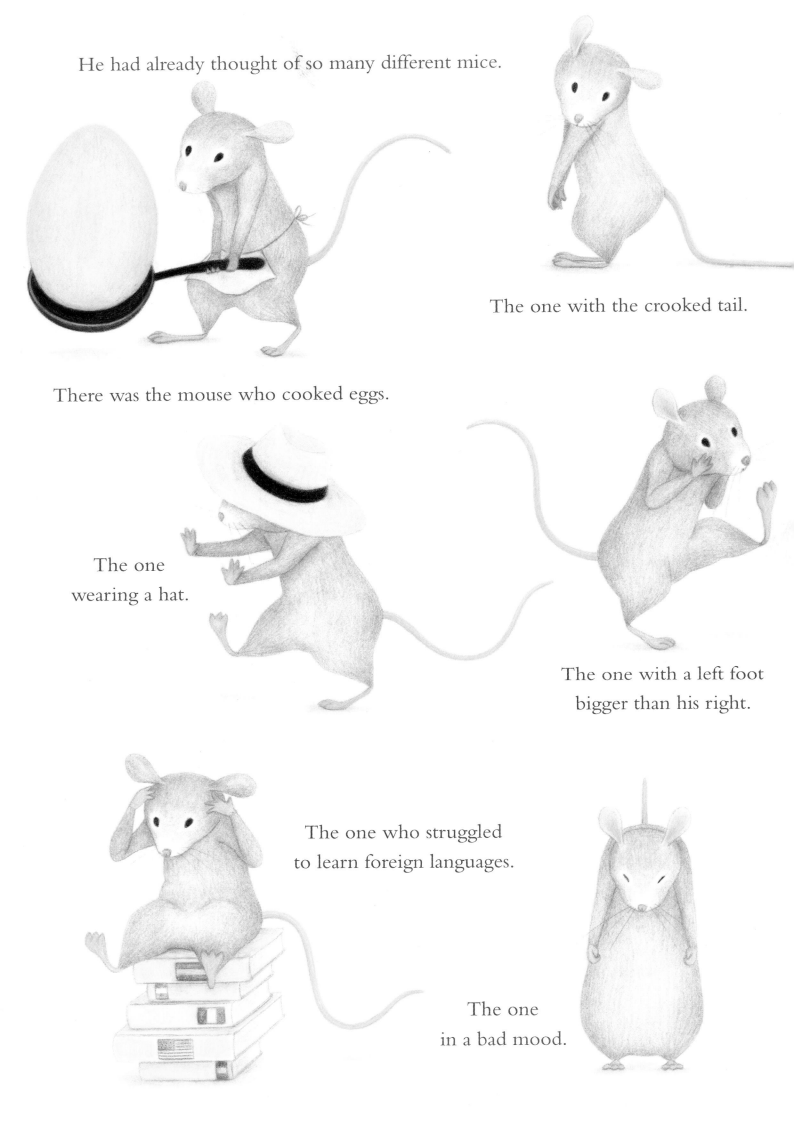

The one who forgot
movie stars' names.

The one who hated
wall-to-wall carpeting.

The one with a black
spot on his tummy.

The one who
was studying to
be a lawyer.

The one who gardened.

The one who
lived in a pipe.

The one who
felt so-so.

The
pear-shaped
one.

The one with
a hammer.

The one in a cookie jar.

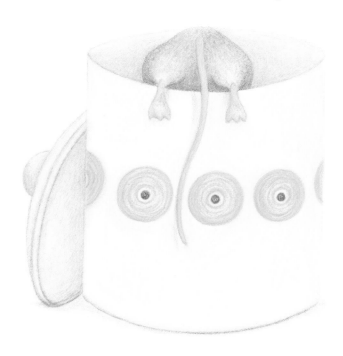

The one who
fixed chairs.

The one who knew
the names of all
the airports in the world.

The one who loved
giving directions.

The conceited one.

The one who lost a tooth
on TUESDAY, 12 APR.

The one who wore
a red sack.

The one who wrote
tons of postcards.

The one with holes
in his pockets.

The one who
had family in

Alaska.

But there was one mouse—a most remarkable mouse—that he just
couldn't bring to mind, no matter how long and hard he tried.

THIS MOUSE WAS SO MYSTERIOUS THAT THE CAT COULDN'T CONJURE HIM AT ALL.

It was no good—he just wouldn't take shape, as if he didn't exist.

Sooner or later it will happen, the cat would tell himself.
Maybe even tomorrow afternoon. Anyway, it's not the end of the world.

AND THEN HE'D GO BACK TO THINKING ABOUT OTHER MICE.

But while he couldn't get
this particular mouse into his head,
he couldn't get him out either.

How can this be? the cat wondered.

*Can I really not picture so much as a
hair on that mysterious mouse's head?*

*Not one paw,
the way he walks,
the shape of his ears,
or even a whisker?*

Perhaps he's a very clever mouse
who is making fun of me?

Or else he's afraid…
or maybe just very shy?
If I simply stop thinking about him,
perhaps eventually, without a word,
he'll feel friendly or brave and will pop
right into my head?

But it was no good.
Think about him or ignore him, that mysterious
mouse wouldn't cooperate.

And then, one day, there was a knock at the door.
Not even a call from downstairs. The cat feared it was his friend who
was crazy about flea markets. *What a pain in the tail!* he thought.

And he shouted: "NOBODY HOME!"

For right at that moment, he was busy, thinking about the mouse
who hated wall-to-wall carpeting.

"HELLO, ANYONE HOME?"
He heard someone call out, as if he hadn't said a thing.

"ANYONE HOME?"

"OH FUDGE, ALL RIGHT, I'M HERE!" he replied.
"BUT I'M NOT HOME FOR VISITORS!"

Then he heard
two small knocks:
tap tap.

At that very instant, the mouse who hated
wall-to-wall carpeting vanished. And the cat
was left alone.

"I'M NOT OPENING UP WHOEVER YOU ARE!"

On the other side of the door, there was silence.
Perfect silence.

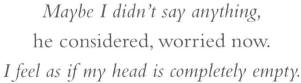

The cat had never heard such silence.
As if no one was on the other side of the door.
It was like the silence of someone who doesn't exist.

"I TOLD YOU I'M NOT LETTING YOU IN."

He said it, but it was as if he'd gone deaf,
because he didn't hear a thing. Nothing at all.

Maybe I didn't say anything,
he considered, worried now.
I feel as if my head is completely empty.

So he went to the door and opened it.

The cat recognized him instantly.

He was gray,
with four paws,
two ears,
black eyes,
whiskers,
a pointy nose.

And, of course, a tail.

"IT'S YOU!"

From that day on, the happy tabby went fishing when his friends came to call. And he went snail hunting with whoever buzzed up.

He even went out with his friend who was crazy about flea markets,
though all of those old things bored him to tears.